The Three Little Pigs

D1395908

Illustration Giuseppe Di Lernia
Written and retold by Clare Lloyd
Designer Charlotte Jennings
Creative director Helen Senior
Publishing director Sarah Larter
Producer John Casey
Senior Pre-Producer Nikoleta Parasaki

First published in Great Britain in 2019 by
Dorling Kindersley Limited
One Embassy Gardens, 8 Viaduct Gardens,
London, SW11 7BW

A CIP catalogue record for this book
is available from the British Library.
ISBN: 978-0-2413-5096-6

Printed and bound in China

For the curious
www.dk.com

MIX
Paper from
responsible sources
FSC™ C018179

This book was made with Forest
Stewardship Council™ certified paper –
one small step in DK's commitment to a
sustainable future. For more information
go to www.dk.com/our-green-pledge

Notes for Parents and Carers

Here are some ideas for discussing important themes in *The Three Little Pigs* with young children. Use these notes to prompt discussion during and after reading the book.

• Which of the three houses in the story would you most like to live in? Why? Which of the little pigs worked hard to build a strong house? Think of a time when you worked hard.

• The third little pig builds a home that will keep him safe from the Big Bad Wolf. What does the third little pig do to make sure his house is strong and safe? Talk about why it is a good idea to take time and care to do things well.

• The third little pig lets the other little pigs stay at his house. Discuss why helping each other is important.

On the edge of a beautiful forest lived a mummy pig, a daddy pig, and three little pigs. The time had come for the three little pigs to leave home.

"Watch out for the Big Bad Wolf!" warned the daddy pig as he waved goodbye.

The three little pigs hadn't walked very far when the first little pig grew tired.

"This will do," yawned the lazy little pig. He found some straw nearby and quickly built his house.

It wasn't long before the second little pig stopped walking and looked around her.

"This will do," she said, and swiftly built a house from the sticks and branches that were scattered around her.

The third little pig walked on, and on, and on. Finally, he found a pretty field by a flowing stream. It was the perfect place to build his house.

The third little pig decided to build a strong brick house to keep him safe from the wolf.

He drew plans...

...he bought the best bricks he could find...

...and finally, after weeks of hard work...

...he stood back and admired his beautiful new home.

Meanwhile, the hungry Big Bad Wolf came across the first little pig and his house of straw.

"Little pig, little pig, let me come in," said the wolf.

"Not by the hair on my chinny-chin-chin!" cried the first little pig.

"Then I'll huff, and I'll puff, and I'll blow your house down!" howled the angry wolf.

So the Big Bad Wolf huffed and he puffed...

...and the tiny straw house came tumbling down!

The little pig ran as fast as he could until he arrived at the house made of sticks.

The Big Bad Wolf snuck up to the house. "Little pigs, little pigs, let me come in!" he growled.

"Not by the hairs on our chinny-chin-chins!" cried the frightened little pigs.

"Then I'll huff, and I'll puff, and I'll blow your house down!" howled the angry wolf.

So the Big Bad Wolf huffed and he puffed...

...and the wobbly stick house came tumbling down!

The two little pigs ran on, and on, and on, until they finally reached the third little pig's house.

"Don't worry! We are safe in my strong brick house," said the third little pig. They heard a bang at the door.

"Little pigs, little pigs, let me come in,"
said a familiar voice. It was the wolf.

"Not by the hairs on
our chinny-chin-chins!"
cried the three little pigs.

"Then I'll huff, and I'll puff, and I'll blow your house down!" howled the angry wolf.

So the Big Bad Wolf huffed and he puffed and he puffed and he huffed...

...but nothing happened.
The house didn't even wobble!

The wolf was furious and VERY hungry. He climbed up to the roof and jumped down the chimney... splash!

The wolf fell in a pot of boiling hot soup and burnt his long, furry tail on the fire! He leapt out of the chimney and ran away as quickly as he could.

As for the little pigs, they lived happily ever after in their house made of bricks. They never ever saw the Big Bad Wolf again.